BALANCING ACT

Distributed in Canada by H. B. Fenn and Company Ltd.

Library of Congress Cataloging-in-Publication Data
has been applied for.

ISBN: 978-0-7534-6192-1

Kingfisher books are available for special promotions and premiums.
For details contact: Director of Special Markets, Holtzbrinck Publishers.

First American Edition August 2008
Printed in India
2 4 6 8 10 9 7 5 3 1
1TR/0408/THOM/SCHOY/60BNWP/C

BALANCING ACT

DONNA KING

KINGFISHER
NEW YORK

Chapter 1

"Bye, Carli!"

"See you Monday!"

"Miss you already!"

Carli Carroll's friends leaned out of the school bus and waved happily. She walked toward the jeep belonging to the Triple X Ranch.

"Hey." Her dad's welcome following her trip to gymnastics camp in Breckenridge was brief and to the point, as always. "Throw your bags in the back. Let's get out of here."

"Hi, Dad. Good to see you, Dad. I missed you, too, Dad," Carli muttered.

"Yeah, yeah, cut out the smart-aleck stuff," Don Carroll replied as he climbed into the cab and turned the ignition. "I've got a heap of work to do at the ranch. How about knuckling down and helping, instead of giving me a hard time?"

"Sorry," Carli said, staring ahead as her dad turned the jeep off the main road and headed along the familiar dirt track toward home. *Bump—rattle—roll*. Tall redwoods lined the narrow road. Way down below, at the base of the steep, rocky mountainside, the clear green water in Silverfish Creek ran high and fast. "How's Mom?" she asked.

"She's good. Getting ready for a big week next week. Twenty-three guests. This week we only have eighteen."

Rattle—rattle. The jeep swayed close to the edge of the track. Suddenly a mule deer leaped out of the undergrowth. Carli's dad swerved toward the rock face and then righted the vehicle. "Darn critter," he muttered.

"I got the 'Best Gymnast' award," Carli mentioned at the Five-Mile Post, which, considering that she was up against gymnasts from throughout Colorado, was a pretty big deal. "By the end of the week, I got to work on the hardest moves for my routines."

Don Carroll glanced sideways at his daughter. "Don't go getting ideas," he warned. "Your mom and me can't afford to send you to gymnastics camp all the time as well as paying for your lessons."

"I never asked you to."

"Well, don't."

Welcome home, Carli. We're real proud of you. She played a silent game, imagining any normal parent's response. *We always knew you were a born horsewoman, but now it turns out you're an exceptionally talented gymnast, too!*

Aw, shucks! she would say modestly in her alternative apple-pie, rosy-cheeked universe. *It ain't nothing!*

Maybe you're not the sharpest tool in the box, her dad would say with a kind smile. *But, honey, you sure are the real thing when it comes to sports!*

"I brought in that chestnut two-year-old from Marshy Meadow," her dad told her instead. "I figure she's ready to sack out."

Carli knew which foal he meant—she'd been there at the birth, when the mare had been in trouble. They'd called in the vet, but the mare had died anyway. Carli had hand raised the foal, which she'd named Diamond. She also knew that her dad's method of schooling the young horse would involve some pretty harsh handling. "I'll do it," she offered quickly.

The Triple X was in sight, nestling in the valley bottom, its pastures strung out beside the creek. Log cabins where the guests stayed were perched on the rocky slopes. The main house stood on the green valley floor.

"Okay," Don agreed. "Ben and I will keep an eye on you. Tomorrow's Saturday. Take Diamond into the round pen before breakfast."

"Oh, but . . ." Saturday was Carli's

gymnastics day, when she went into Colorado Springs for training, and he knew it. But she'd been in Breckenridge for a whole week. Better not push it. "Okay," she agreed. "Tomorrow first thing. I'll be there."

"She's pretty," Lee remarked as Carli worked Diamond in the round pen. "I like the white star on her forehead."

As the newest wrangler on the ranch, Lee had drawn the short straw and had been up since before dawn, bringing horses in from the pastures to saddle them up, ready for dude action. Now he sat on the rail, watching Carli work.

Carli snaked a rope along the ground, close behind the young chestnut's hindquarters. It sent her forward at a canter, head up and mane flying in the wind. Diamond kept to the edge of the round pen, staying ahead of the rope.

"I'm waiting for her head to go down," Carli explained. "Then she'll stop running and turn to me. Look, she's doing it now."

Diamond slowed to a trot and lowered her head.

"She's been running a long time, and now she's tired. She's thinking, *Okay, boss, what do you want me to do now?* In other words, she's submitting."

"Neat!" Lee watched closely. "Can I try that?"

"Sure. Send her around the pen counterclockwise." Carli handed over the rope and then hopped up onto the rail. "My dad likes to tie a sack around the hindquarters and make them run—calls it 'sacking out.' But it scares the heck out of them. I prefer this method."

She glanced at her watch as the wrangler took over. Eight-thirty. She'd skipped breakfast and had been working with Diamond for more than an hour, which meant that she could finish now and still get to her class in the Springs on time.

"Who's driving into town this morning?"

she asked Lee.

He snaked the rope at Diamond's heels and made her break into a canter around the pen. "Me," he told her. "I need to pick up some antibiotics from the vet."

Carli nodded. "Can I hitch a ride?"

"Sure thing." Lee stopped, driving Diamond forward the second he saw her lower her head. "Easy, there! Good girl!"

"What time?"

"Nine. I'll finish up here with the filly if you need to get ready."

"Thanks, Lee." Carli grabbed the chance. "Can you put Diamond in with the mares and foals and give her extra grain? I'll meet you in half an hour!"

She had 30 minutes to shower and change into clean jeans and a T-shirt, to grab her leotard and make herself a quick peanut-butter sandwich that she could eat during the ride into town.

"How long did you work with the filly?"

her mom asked, coming into the kitchen just as Carli was packing her snack.

Beth Carroll was the same as her husband—short on the hugs and hellos, long on the silences. She was small and thin, with lines on her face that showed she'd lived out in the sun and wind. And she wore the full Western uniform— cowboy boots, jeans, and a plaid shirt, with her long, dark hair tied back.

"An hour or more," Carli answered. "She's doing great. Next time I'll do the join up and try putting a saddle on her."

"Nice work," Beth said quietly. She noticed Carli's gymnastics bag on the kitchen floor and frowned. Carli cringed, waiting for her mother to comment on it. "I was hoping maybe you'd stick around this morning and help with the cabins."

"I'll do it when I get back," Carli promised. "I need to go 'cause I have to tell Lorene about everything that happened while I was away on my gymnastics trip."

Beth went tightlipped and sniffy. "Life wasn't exactly a breeze around here while you were gone. We were pretty short of help."

How to make a girl feel bad! Her parents could write a book on the subject. "Leave the cabins. I'll do them," she promised again, grabbing her bag before her mom could stop her. "Lee's giving me a ride— he'll be waiting. Gotta go!"

Today Lorene, the gymnastics coach, was concentrating on the vaulting horse.

"Come off that springboard like you're launching yourself into outer space!" she told her students. "It has to be explosive from the get-go. Bang—onto the board and off with all the propulsion you can get!"

Carli was working on her specialty—a piked vault with one and a half twists. The springboard had to launch her onto the vaulting table in a handspring, from where she could bound off again in an upward arc, traveling as far and as fast as she could to allow time for the pike and twists.

"You next, Carli!" Lorene yelled. "Stick your landing this time—no extra steps!"

Carli raised herself up to her full height and took a deep breath. She began her run-up with a skip and then a fast sprint. Ahead was the springboard and the vaulting table. Beyond that, a soft landing. Lorene stood to one side so that she could watch the movement of every muscle in her gymnasts' bodies. She never missed a thing.

Carli's dark, wavy hair was tucked back in a tight ponytail. It bobbed as she sprinted for the springboard. *Bang!* Her feet hit the springboard, and she bounced up. She executed a perfect handspring from the vaulting table, flying up and folding into piked position, rotating out of it, and landing with two feet on the mat. No steps, no wobbles.

"Perfect!" Lorene called. "Now, Gina, your turn!"

Cool! Carli told herself. She jogged back to join the line. *Totally cool, in fact!*

She loved riding—she'd loped out to some great spots on horseback. Speed was Carli's thing, plus the balance and agility that you needed in order to ride well. Then there was the sound of the horse's hooves thundering across green meadows, the fallen logs to jump, the crouching, swerving, and bending to avoid low branches. All good.

But the thrill of hitting that springboard and throwing yourself at the table, of soaring into the air and perfecting your salto or your pike, of having only yourself, pure muscle and bone and determination, to rely on—that was something else.

Carli stood in line, breathing deeply, going through the next vault in her mind, rehearsing every movement.

"Good job, Gina. Great height there.

Good vault. You're next, Tanya. Watch your run-up. Come on, girl, focus. Get ready and go!"

Nothing compares! Carli thought. *Give me the balance beam and the uneven bars, the vault, and the floor exercises over horseback riding any day!*

Chapter 2

"It's okay—I'm used to hard work," Carli told Lee.

It was Sunday morning, and he'd found her lifting bales of hay onto the back of the jeep and offered to help.

"Anyway, don't you have your own chores?" she asked with a grin.

Lee nodded. "Yeah, to help you put the hay in the feeders. Don's orders."

"Oh!" Carli's grin widened. "In that case, you lift while I stack."

Springing quickly from the tailgate onto the metal platform, she took the bales from Lee and hauled them up. When they'd finished, she clambered over the hay and swung into the cab, sitting beside Lee as he started the engine.

"Hold on!" he yelled.

"Whoa!" she cried, hanging on tight as Lee drove the ancient truck from the barn out into the pastures. "What is this—the Indy Five Hundred?"

Thirty horses came cantering for food. There were chestnuts and bays, grays and palominos, all crowding around to get at their feed. They munched greedily as Carli and Lee tossed hay into the metal feeders.

"So, Lee—where's home for you?" Carli asked as they drove the empty truck back to the barn.

"Chicago. But I came here for a year before college, to be with my dad."

Carli thought for a second, figuring it out. "Okay, so your dad lives here in Colorado and your mom lives in Chicago?"

He nodded. "I'm a city boy. My dad and mom split up when I was six years old. My dad drifted awhile and then landed here."

"Where exactly?" Carli thought that Lee

seemed cool—kind of shy, which she liked, and serious.

"In the Springs. I drive into town and see him on my days off."

"And how does a city boy like you like working on a ranch?"

Lee thought for a while. "I'm happy working with horses."

"But not with people?" she guessed.

He grinned and ducked his head. "I never said that. How about you, Carli? Do you like the ranch life?"

She paused. "Same as you. The animals are cool. But, anyway, I have to go clean cabins now." Stepping down from the jeep, she turned back to Lee. "Later on I'm going to work with Diamond in the round pen. Come join us if you have time."

"I'd like that," he said quietly. "But Don asked me to lead a kids' trail ride this afternoon. Sorry."

"No problem—see you around." Carli headed for the laundry room to pick up fresh sheets. She had six cabins to clean and 15 beds to make before the new guests arrived at three o'clock. Then she had a date with Diamond. After that, she had to catch up on all the studying she'd missed because of gymnastics camp.

"Hey, Carli!" Tanya called her at five-thirty. "Is there any chance you can make it into town tonight? Lorene says she can fit in an extra coaching session."

"No way!" Carli said, staring at the stack of textbooks on the table. "We've got twenty-three new guests in, and I've been making beds all afternoon. I haven't even started my math homework. It's crazy here."

"Poor you," her friend commiserated.

Carli looked out her bedroom window, at Lee and her dad stacking more hay onto the jeep, at the horses grazing in the meadows, and the mountains rising sheer out of the valley. In the distance, Sawtooth Lake glittered under a pink evening sun. "Yeah, it's a tough life," she said, half joking, half serious. "I'll tell you one thing for sure, Tanya—I'm coming to school tomorrow so I can have a break!"

Monday, and school was school—the same as always.

"... Carli Carroll, I want to see your math homework. Please hand it in first thing tomorrow morning."

"... You need to improve your grades in history, Carli. With a little more effort, I'm sure you can do it."

"... Hey, Carli. Want to play tennis?"

School had ended, and Carli and Tanya were getting ready to ride across town to the gym. "Sorry, Matt, I have gymnastics tonight. Maybe tomorrow," she replied. Matt was really nice, but gymnastics had to come first as far as Carli was concerned.

They pedaled out through the school gates and rode across the parking lot toward the nearby mall. Taking a shortcut, they arrived at the same time as their friend Gina and a new girl named Martha. They all went into the changing rooms together, chatting about the session ahead.

"Lorene wants us to work on the beam today," Tanya told them.

Gina groaned. "She wants me to work on my split jump, and I'm not up to that right now. I twisted my ankle."

"Tell her," Carli insisted. "Lorene's not a monster. She'll understand."

Some of the girls were scared of the coach, but not Carli. Sure, Lorene had a tough exterior and a voice like a drill sergeant. And she hardly ever cracked a smile. But Carli knew that it was a front—all Lorene ever wanted to do was help you reach your true potential as a gymnast.

"I can't tell her. She'll say I'm wimping out, especially since we've got the interstate competition in Denver coming up soon," Gina said with a sigh. She flexed her sore ankle and then followed the others into the gym.

"Lorene sure seems fierce!" Martha muttered to Carli, hanging back. She'd spotted the coach dishing out orders to a bunch of girls who'd arrived before them.

"I want you out of your comfort zones, pushing your bodies just that little bit harder," the coach was insisting in her loud voice. "I know the balance beam is only four inches wide, but you have to attack it as if you're working on a floor exercise. You must be confident up there."

"She's not so fierce when you get to know her," Carli told Martha with a grin. "Come on, don't be scared."

Lorene turned to greet them. "Hey, girls. Come join us! Gina, what's up?"

"Nothing. I'm okay."

Lorene studied Gina closely. "You're limping. What happened?"

"See, she spots the littlest thing!" Carli told the new girl.

"I twisted my ankle playing basketball," Gina confessed.

Lorene nodded. "Okay, so sit this one out. Do some sit-ups, work on your upper body strength, but don't put any strain on that ankle until you've seen the physical therapist. In fact, Rick's in the treatment room, so go and do that right now!"

Relieved, Gina zipped up her top and limped away. Meanwhile, Lorene began her pep talk all over again.

"The balance beam—more than sixteen feet of leather-covered sprung wood, four feet above the floor, ninety seconds to impress the judges. It's a tough discipline and one you need to master if you're going to place at the interstate competition."

Let me get up there! Carli thought as Lorene coached.

"Tanya, when you work on your routine today, I want you to focus on covering the entire sixteen-foot length of the beam. You'll lose points if you don't. Martha, why don't you get up there first and show us what you can do? Are you okay with that?"

Nodding anxiously, Martha went forward. Once on the beam, she drew up her slight body to full height, balanced on one skinny leg, and went into a slow arabesque. Then she tilted backward, arched her back, and executed a backflip, followed by a lunge and a pivot, which threw her sideways into a bad wobble.

Lorene quickly stepped forward in case Martha fell. "Okay?"

Martha nodded, breathed deep, and took off from one foot into a graceful cat leap.

"She's got guts," Tanya said to Carli. "How old do you think she is? Younger than us—maybe eleven?"

Carli nodded. *Let me up there!* Eager to begin, she thought her way through her own beam routine—the cat leaps and the pivots, the body wave leading to a back handspring and then a back salto.

And today she wanted to include the extra 360-degree turn that she'd been working on during her gymnastics trip. That would be a challenge—to fit it into the 90-second time limit and make it flow with her routine.

"Okay, good!" Lorene told Martha, who dismounted from the beam and breathlessly awaited the verdict. "That's a challenging routine, Martha—plenty for us to work on together."

The blond kid's face lit up with relief. She nodded and trotted back to join the line.

"Okay, Carli, I can see you chomping at the bit over there," Lorene said. She gestured her forward. "Up you go!"

My turn! My chance to get it right! Let this be perfect!

Carli ran forward and vaulted onto the beam. She landed, and the moment her bare feet touched the cool, polished surface, she felt at home. Like a tightrope walker, she stretched out her arms and then drew them up over her head. *Attack the beam!* she thought. *Show no fear. Imagine you're performing your floor exercises.*

She arched forward into a slow, smooth handspring, then progressed from there into a quick salto—flipping head over heels. Then, with a twist of the upper body, she made a 180-degree turn into a cabriole leap—which wasn't quite high enough—and then spun into a cartwheel.

Believe! Carli told herself. *Forget the messed-up cabriole, focus on the new three-sixty-degree turn. Look ahead!*

She went on working, kept control, stretching every fiber in her body, flexing every muscle. *Bend, twist, balance. Leap, land, and turn.* Everything here had to do with balance, keeping it together, and not letting go. She nailed the 360, but she had to rush through the middle section of her routine, conscious of the seconds ticking away.

Then, finally, Carli was at the end of her routine and ending with a split jump into a forward flip with a twist. She made a safe landing, head back, arms upstretched.

"Good work." Lorene's comment came with a "but," and Carli waited for her to continue. "Not sure about the extra turn.

Let's think about it."

Tough love! Carli gritted her teeth and nodded. The coach had 30 years of experience. Lorene had seen it all and done it all herself—she'd even competed at Olympic level.

"Okay, Tanya, you're up!"

"How did you do?" Gina asked Carli at the end of the session. She was still in the treatment room with the physical therapist, having her ankle treated.

"Pretty good, except for my cabriole. That wasn't a hundred percent."

Gina grinned. "There's Little Miss Perfectionist for you!"

"Tell that to my math teacher!" Carli laughed. She stayed there for a while, watching the physical therapist gently tilt and flex Gina's injured ankle. He was a new guy at the gym—gray haired but still in good shape, clean-shaven, and wearing a black T-shirt and sweatpants. "How's the ankle?" Carli asked Gina.

"Sore. Not too bad. Rick says I need to rest it for a week, which is such a bummer."

"Minimum," the physical therapist emphasized, giving her a stern look. "I'll see you again on Wednesday," he said, motioning for Gina to put her shoe back on.

"Hey, Rick, this is Carli Carroll." Gina made the introductions. "She's the best gymnast around here."

"Hi, Carli," Rick said, turning his back to her to stuff some used towels into a laundry basket.

"Rick isn't exactly a talker," Gina explained as she and Carli left the room. "I got about fifty words out of him the whole time I was in there, and forty of them were grunts."

Carli smiled. "Hey, I came to offer you a ride home. Lee's picking me up. We could drive your way."

"Ooh, Lee!" Gina giggled. "Is he the cute guy who drove you into town?"

"He's my dad's new wrangler." Carli blushed and played down Lee's good looks. "He gets all the menial jobs, like driving into town to pick me up."

"Yeah, *and* he's cute!" Gina insisted.

"And you're *walking* home if you don't stop fooling around." Carli searched the parking lot for the Triple X jeep. She spotted the dusty brown wreck and then realized that there was no driver. "Where's Lee?"

"Back there." Gina pointed over her shoulder toward the exit to the gym. "That's him, isn't it?"

Sure enough, Lee was leaning against the doorjamb with his hands in his pockets, deep in conversation with Rick, the noncommunicative physical therapist.

Both men seemed animated. Lee kept on asking questions, which the older man brushed aside. Rick was spreading his palms out flat and shrugging in a don't-ask-me way.

Why are they so friendly? Carli wondered.

"Do they know each other?" Gina asked.

"I don't know. Still think he's cute?" Carli asked as Lee suddenly turned away and strode across the lot toward them.

"Hey, girls," he said, nodding shyly.

"Lee, can we give Gina a ride out to Redwood Park? It's on our way home."

"Sure thing," he replied. He seemed reluctant to talk as Gina and Carli piled into the cab.

"So, what's Lorene planning for Wednesday?" Gina asked. "Bars or floor exercise?"

"Floor," Carli answered, sinking into her seat and strapping herself in.

"Pity. I could've worked on the bars, even with this ankle." Like Carli, Gina was very eager. "Now it looks like I'll fall behind in my training program. I might not make the interstate competition this summer after all."

"Yeah, you will," Carli insisted. "We both will!"

"*You* will; I *so* know you will!" Gina sighed, pushing her short, dark hair back from her forehead. "Like I was telling Rick, you're the best junior gymnast in all of the Springs, probably even including Denver."

Mention of the physical therapist's name seemed to bring a frown to Lee's face, but he drove on without comment.

Gina chatted on. "I told Rick he should take a look at you, Carli."

Carli shrugged. For the first time she noticed that Lee was uncomfortable with their conversation. She decided to charge in with her usual directness. "Hey, Lee, I didn't realize you knew Rick until I saw you two talking back there!"

Lee shrugged and turned onto the Redwood Park road.

"Stop here. This is my house!" Gina cried. She opened the door and jumped out of the cab.

"Remember that ankle!" Carli cried.

"Ouch!"

"Too late."

"See you tomorrow," Gina said with a

wave, limping away.

Quickly, Lee backed up into a driveway and turned the jeep around. Soon they were back on the highway.

"So how do you know him?" Carli persisted.

"Who?" Lee checked his mirror.

"Rick," Carli said. "You *know* who!"

"Sure I know him," Lee conceded, speeding along the side of the clear river. Up ahead, the road rose steeply into the snowcapped mountains.

"How?" Getting facts out of Lee was like prying crayfish meat out of its shell. "Rick only just started working at the gym. So what's the link?"

Lee glanced sideways and narrowed his blue eyes, deciding to satisfy Carli's curiosity at last. "The link is—Rick Scottsdale is my father."

"Your *father*!" she echoed.

Lee nodded. "Yeah. Is that specific enough for you?"

Chapter 3

Lee and Rick Scottsdale—it was obviously a touchy subject, and Carli avoided it when she got up early the next morning to school Diamond in the round pen.

"You want to watch me do the join up?" she asked Lee when she spotted him saddling horses in the corral.

On the tack-room porch, Carli's dad and the head wrangler, Ben Adams, were matching up names of guests beside the names of horses—Jennie Foster next to Gunsmoke, Art Foster next to Forrest Gump, and so on. They were getting ready to send the guests out for a ride, and Lee was working flat out.

"I'll come over as soon I've finished

here," Lee promised.

So Carli led the chestnut filly into the pen and then let her off the halter rein. She sent her cantering around the edge of the pen, waiting for her to lower her head. "Good girl," she murmured. "You learn fast."

Diamond's head went down sooner than before. Then she turned in toward Carli, waiting for her next move.

Carli stood patiently, avoiding eye contact, expecting the filly to approach in her own time.

Diamond looked long and hard at the still figure in the center of the pen. She flicked her ears and sniffed the air and then gingerly took a step toward Carli.

Out of the corner of her eye, Carli noticed her dad and Ben come up to the fence to watch, but she didn't take her attention off the filly, not even for a second. *Come on, Diamond, I'm not gonna hurt you!* she thought. *You can trust me, I promise!*

Perhaps the young horse remembered

the early days when Carli had hand raised her and cared for her after her mom had died. In any case, she came smoothly forward, neck stretched out, nostrils quivering.

"Good girl!" Carli breathed.

Diamond was only a step away, growing bolder by the second. When Carli slowly raised her arm, she shied for a fraction of a second but then held steady while Carli reached out to stroke her face.

"Easy, girl. You're so good. I'm just gonna fasten this halter on—you know what it is; you've worn it before. Yeah, good girl!"

With the rope halter on and the filly nuzzling up to her, Carli knew that her morning's job was done. Diamond had joined up.

"Nice work!" Lee called from the fence. He'd joined the other two men to watch Carli work with Diamond.

"Don't you believe it," Don Carroll muttered as he moved off with Ben. "Carli's newfangled technique takes way too long. I go for the good old sacking-out method—tie a sack on their backs and run 'em into the ground till they can't move no more. Then slap a saddle on 'em."

"Yeah, thanks, Dad!" Carli stood up to him. "That's *so* not the modern way!"

"I was impressed," Lee admitted. "I figure Carli . . ."

"Yeah, well, go and be impressed back in the tack room." Don cut him short. "There's bridles to clean and fit before the guests come down."

Working with Diamond, standing up to her dad, driving into town, drifting through the school day and then back home to more ranch work—this was Carli's routine Monday and Tuesday.

"You're getting more than your fair share of driving me into town," she said to Lee on Wednesday morning. "You must be bored out of your mind with this route."

"It's okay," Lee told her. "Anyway, today's

my day off. I get to stay in town and hang out."

"With your dad?" she asked. She opened her mouth, and the question fell out without her brain kicking in. *Touchy subject, remember.*

"Maybe," Lee grunted. "I've got errands to run. I might see a movie."

"But you'll be there to drive me home after my gymnastics class?" Carli checked. "I should be finished at six-thirty, if that's okay."

Lee pulled up at the school gates. "See you then," he said. "Have a good day."

"I *won't*!" she assured him. "At least not until I get out on that gym floor!"

The floor exercise was the high point of gymnastics for Carli—the pinnacle, the peak, the spot where everything came together. On the floor she could dance— really dance. She could be the acrobat. She could be herself!

Her music began. The violins jumped and

jigged as Carli sprang into action with a series of handsprings combined with Cossack leaps and pivots across the diagonal. They were high-speed, medium-difficulty moves, still building momentum.

Rick Scottsdale joined Lorene in the gym, watching Carli's performance.

"Good energy," he said. "Good sense of rhythm."

Carli stopped at the very edge of the floor, stretched both arms high, and as the music continued to race, she went into a body wave and then a series of quick steps into a half-in, half out salto, giving a half twist on each flip—down into a plié as the music calmed down and a deep cello took over from the violins—a relevé, slow and graceful, another pivot, and a slow walkover, walking through the air as her hands took her weight.

"Carli is very supple," Lorene said. "And strong. Good control. For sure, she's got what it takes."

Carli's momentum was still building; she

was traveling low across the floor, waiting for those soaring violins to return. *Now for the three connected saltos—up, head over heels, and twist, again and again! Turn and tumble this way. Turn again and tumble.* She ran at the triple twist—the climax—gathering speed, aiming to rotate her whole body three times in the air, flinging herself into it, spinning and landing in perfect balance.

"Brave," Rick said to Lorene. "The girl has guts."

Winding down, turning and tilting, putting in leaps and pirouettes, ending with a split leap and down onto both knees, arms outstretched.

Breathless, smiling—free!

Rick nodded and disappeared into the treatment room.

After the class, Lorene collared Carli. "Did you pinpoint any faults in your routine tonight?" she asked.

"No—at least not in the execution. My

rhythm was okay, too." Carli zipped up her jacket and thrust her legs into her sweatpants. "How about my presentation? Did you see anything?"

"Me, personally? No, I didn't," Lorene said slowly, as if a new idea had occurred to her. "But how would you like an expert opinion?"

Carli smiled. "That would be you, Lorene, wouldn't it?"

"Okay, then—another expert opinion. If you don't mind, I'd like you to come with me."

"Lead the way."

Still puzzled, Carli followed the coach out of the gym, past the door to the shower room, along a corridor stacked with equipment and weights, until they came to the treatment room.

Lorene knocked on the door. "Rick, can we come in?"

There was a short pause before the physical therapist opened the door. He didn't let them enter the room, but stood barring their way. "What is it, Lorene? I'm busy writing up case notes."

"This won't take long, Rick. I know you had some comments on Carli's performance when we were watching her floor exercise earlier. Do you have any advice for her?"

Carli couldn't help frowning. What could Rick Scottsdale possibly know about women's gymnastics that Lorene hadn't already covered?

The physical therapist's face showed no reaction. His thin lips stayed set in a straight line, and his blue eyes were fixed on the floor. "You don't need my advice, Lorene," he muttered. "You know what you're doing better than anyone I can think of. Always did."

"But a fresh eye is good," the coach insisted. "Carli would really appreciate it if you gave your opinion."

I would? Carli thought. This was only her third time seeing Rick Scottsdale. So far, she wasn't particularly impressed.

Rick shrugged and glanced briefly at

Carli. He seemed to catch the hostility in her eyes and looked back at her with a little more interest.

"Rick was on the U.S. team with me at the Montreal Olympics, way back in seventy-six," Lorene explained to Carli. "He was a total genius on the rings. That's why I invited him here to work as a physical therapist."

Carli's jaw dropped. No way had she expected this. The Olympic Games in 1976 were the golden games—when Nadia Comaneci, Carli's all-time heroine, had scored her perfect tens. And Lorene was telling her that Rick had been a part of all that!

"So come on, Rick, tell us what you saw in Carli's performance," Lorene invited.

"Challenging routine." He shrugged, still reluctant to cooperate. "Who did the choreography?"

"I did," Lorene answered. "But Carli figured out her own strengths—especially the flowing energy she builds up in the middle section. She has natural grace, don't you think?"

Rick nodded. "I'd pick out the slow walkover—that was as good as it gets. Variety in the routine was good. The triple twist was way up there at international level."

Carli stared at the gray-haired ex-gymnast. Although his voice was flat and his expression gave nothing away, he had obviously been paying attention, as he was picking out the highlights of her routine.

"We'd like to know how you rated the overall presentation and artistry." Lorene wouldn't let Rick off the hook just yet. She wanted to squeeze every scrap of advice out of him.

And now Rick did look Carli straight in the eye. "Still some work needed there," he said bluntly.

"Hmm." At last Lorene had pinned him down.

"What kind of work?" Carli asked quickly. If there was anything that needed improvement, she wanted to know.

"You have to let your personality come through," Rick told her. "Right now, you're way too serious. You need more bounce."

"Bounce . . . right!" Lorene said, as if she suddenly saw what he was saying.

Unexpectedly, Rick's criticism stung Carli. She frowned and looked down before mumbling a farewell to her coach and heading for the door.

"Right on target, as usual, Rick," Lorene confirmed, watching Carli turn and walk back down the corridor, her head hanging. "I'll say this for you—you may be down on your luck right now, old friend, but you've still got the best eye in the business!"

"You never said your dad was a gymnast," Carli said to Lee during the ride home. She was still feeling upset about the negative comment regarding her presentation.

"You never asked," Lee replied. "Anyhow, it was a long time ago. Way before I was born."

"Lorene says he was good."

Lee shrugged. He stopped at the gas station to refuel. When he came back, he handed Carli a pack of gum. "So how's Diamond coming along?" he asked.

"She's doing good." Carli clocked the change of subject and took the hint. "I'll use the round pen to put a saddle on her early tomorrow morning."

Lee nodded. "I hope I'll be there. I like the way you work with the horses, Carli. I think being a horse trainer would be a pretty good job for you when you finish school."

"Yeah, but it isn't what I want. Gymnastics is my thing. It's all I've ever wanted to do since I was eight years old."

They rode on in silence, turning off onto the dirt road, catching glimpses of Silverfish Creek between the trees.

"But how long does it last?" Lee asked after a long silence.

"How long does *what* last?"

"Being a top gymnast. A couple of years—

three or four if you're lucky. Then what?"

To Carli, the answer was obvious. "Then you learn to be a judge or a coach. You stay involved. Listen, Lee—you think training horses would be good? Well, I happen to believe that training young gymnasts would be better. Like Lorene. She has a cool life."

"Yeah? What if you can't stay involved? Not everyone can be a coach. What if you have to drop out?"

Why the third degree? Carli wondered. How come shy Lee was ramming the questions down her throat? "Like your dad, you mean?"

Lee nodded. "He was the top man on the rings, yet I look at him now and I worry about him. He doesn't have any direction in his life."

"I get you," Carli said, respecting Lee's silence as the jeep jolted over the rutted surface and past the Five-Mile Post. Lee didn't reply, and Carli sat back, looking out the window.

Chapter 4

"You were flying today, Carli." Gina picked up her towel after practicing her routine on the uneven bars. "Those release moves were really something."

"Thanks." Carli felt happy with her Saturday morning's work. "How's your ankle?"

"Much better. I have to see Rick now for another treatment, but I could meet up with you and Tanya later if you want to grab a snack."

"Speaking of Rick . . . " Tanya came up behind them and pointed out the physical therapist standing in the doorway, apparently waiting for Gina. "How come he keeps watching you, Carli?"

Carli was startled. "What do you mean?"

"He was there earlier, while you were on the bars. It was as if he was a judge, scoring your every move. As soon as your routine was over, he moved away."

Carli felt herself stiffen. No doubt the physical therapist had spotted more flaws in her performance. "Believe it or not, he used to compete as an Olympic gymnast," she told them. "In seventy-six, alongside Lorene."

"Wow! You wouldn't think so to look at the guy now." Tanya shook her head. "He seems kind of—boring!"

"Pretty gray—Mr. Average," Gina agreed.

From their huddle by the bars, Tanya looked Rick over. "Mr. *Below* Average. I mean, what is he wearing? That sweatshirt definitely came from a thrift store!"

"*Shh!*" Even though she wasn't a fan of Rick Scottsdale, Carli was uncomfortable with this girlie giggling. When Gina went off with Rick, and Lorene called Carli across, she was glad to escape.

"So, Carli," the coach began "Another excellent morning's work. Neat dismounts, exciting transitions."

Carli nodded and waited for the next piece of analysis from her long-time trainer. Instead, there was silence.

"I've been thinking," Lorene began again after the longest pause. "And I've decided that I've taught you just about all I can in this group situation."

Carli blinked and then tilted her head to one side. "What are you saying?"

"I'm saying you need to move on," Lorene replied, guiding Carli toward the exit. "If you're going to make it to the next level, especially after the competition in Denver, you need one-on-one attention. You need someone to figure out a diet and strength-building program exclusively for you, someone to work to improve the fine details of your routines. I can't do that when I need to work with newcomers like Martha."

Carli frowned, trying to figure out what Lorene was leading up to. Was there an ulterior motive behind her words? What was the hidden agenda? She didn't have to wait long to find out.

"How does this sound to you?" Lorene asked. "How about Rick stepping in and helping me with your coaching from now on? He could do all the stuff I've been talking about."

"*Rick?* " Carli echoed.

"You don't need to decide right away," Lorene said hurriedly. "I'm just floating the idea. Rick hasn't always been a physical therapist. He got his professional coaching certificate way back, so that's not a problem. And trust me—he's an amazing guy. He'd bring out the best in you, without a doubt."

Carli's head was spinning. "This is pretty sudden," she stammered. "I mean, you and I—we've worked together since I was eight. You know me better than anyone."

Lorene nodded. "Sure, and I won't stop working with you. I'll be beside Rick every step of the way. But maybe you and I have gotten too cozy. I think you need to be pushed a little—you know, taken out of your comfort zone. Rick would definitely do that."

"Let me think about it." Carli needed to buy herself some time.

"Sure, no rush. I haven't even spoken to Rick about it yet. And it's a big decision for both of you." There was another long pause, and then Lorene said, "I think you can make it all the way to the top, Carli."

"You do?" Carli's heart flipped and twisted like it was doing a floor exercise all on its own.

"To the very top—to the Olympics and beyond."

"Wow!" A pathetic, little-kid word to convey the excitement that she was feeling, Carli knew.

"If . . ." Lorene said slowly. "*If* you get the

coaching now. If you're pushed and honed, put into the right competitions within the state of Colorado and across the country so that the selectors notice you. You hear what I'm saying?"

Flip-flop went Carli's heart. Her pulse raced.

"So think about it," Lorene said finally.

"I will," Carli promised.

"And let me know on Monday."

The Olympics and beyond! Carli repeated Lorene's words to herself as she worked with Diamond in the round pen. Even now, it made her heart race. It was what she'd dreamed of but never dared put into words—her heart's desire.

"You're so smart, Diamond," she murmured, as the filly did a willing join up. She ran her hands down the horse's smooth neck and through its pale honey mane. "Now, look, I'm going to show you this saddle blanket—I'm just slipping it across your back, no problem!"

Diamond's whole body quivered as she felt the blanket rest across her back. For a few seconds she couldn't understand the weird new sensation.

"Carli, can you come and help in the kitchen when you're through out there?" Beth Carroll called from the porch. "We've got a whole heap of breakfast orders piling up."

The Olympics! But it would mean working with Rick Scottsdale, who she didn't know and who, let's face it, she didn't even like.

"Carli, you heard what your mom said." Don Carroll interrupted her work with Diamond. "You hand that filly over to me now and go help in the kitchen!"

Carli nodded and washed her hands and then started helping with breakfast— making pancakes, cooking bacon until it crisped, serving eggs over easy to a dozen hungry, talkative guests. Then she headed out again to the round pen, to find that her dad had handed Diamond over to Lee.

"Hey, Lee," she said. "You got Diamond's saddle on. That's cool!"

He smiled and nodded. "What next, Miss Horse Trainer?"

"Watch," she told him, stepping up into the nearest stirrup and relaxing her body across Diamond's saddle. "See, she's learning to take my weight, but she's not ready to let me swing a leg over and sit."

Uneasy at yet another fresh sensation, little Diamond skittered sideways, and Carli quickly slipped to the ground. "I guess that's enough pressure for today. Do you want to help me brush her down and then feed her?"

Lee glanced at his watch. "I haven't eaten breakfast yet."

"Oh, okay. I can manage here."

"No, it's cool. I'll skip the food and maybe get it later."

Together, Lee and Carli led Diamond into the corral and began to work with the brushes.

"Hey, Carli, your dad wants you to lead a trail ride this morning!" Ben Adams called from the bunkhouse.

"Cool, no problem!" she yelled back.

She and Lee soon finished grooming Diamond and led her into the feed stall. "Just enough time to pick up a snack!" Carli told him.

So they headed toward the kitchen for a stack of pancakes. "Thanks for your help, Lee," she said, her mouth full.

"No problem."

She looked at him across the table and made a quick decision. After all, who else could she confide in? "Hey, Lee, I hope you don't mind me talking about your dad."

"Again?" Lee said with a wry smile.

"*Again*," she said and nodded. "Sorry. But I have this—what would you call it? This dilemma! And you might be able to help me out."

Lee stopped eating and looked serious. "Go on," he said.

"Your dad—Rick—he used to be a coach, didn't he?"

Lee nodded and said, "Way back, yeah."

"Well, now my trainer, Lorene, thinks your dad should step in and start coaching me one on one."

"She does?" Lee lost interest in his breakfast and stood up to stare out the window.

"She says he would help me get to the very top in gymnastics—and I really, really want that to happen."

"Yeah."

"So I wondered what you thought about the idea. Like, should I take a risk and get the extra coaching? Or should I stick with Lorene?"

"You're asking me to tell you about my dad?" Lee said slowly. He came back to the table and sat down. "Even though you might not like what you hear?"

"Go for it!" she said firmly, wondering what the young ranch hand was going to say.

"Okay. I never saw it for myself, but from what I hear, my dad was a top-class gymnast. But he was a lousy father."

Carli nodded. "I guessed as much."

"He was never there for me," Lee went on. "He was always off on some trip to Wisconsin or Iowa, looking for the next international gold-medal winner. And when he was home, he wasn't interested in Mom or me—not really. He was trying to sell diet supplements and working on training programs all the time, aiming to produce the superman or superwoman who would beat the Russians and the Romanians."

"Did he ever succeed?" Carli asked.

Lee shook his head. "And he never earned any money out of it either. The sport ate him up and spat him out again, without any direction or anything left to live for. But the problem was, he couldn't let go."

"Of what?"

"Of being there, way back in Montreal,

of representing his country and being at the top of his game."

"So he couldn't get past competing in the Olympics?" Carli said, beginning to understand.

Lee frowned and fell silent. "My mom always said that life was a balancing act—like being on the beam and trying not to fall off. One wrong move and you were done. Well, Dad's wrong move was to get hooked on his Olympic memories. For years and years. And every year he earned less—even when I was a little kid, Mom had to work hard to pay the bills."

"So your mom was trying her best to keep it together."

"Yeah. She didn't blame him. But in the end, they broke up. I stayed with Mom. Dad lost everything."

"Because he didn't balance gymnastics with the rest of his life," Carli concluded.

Lee had answered some of her questions, but now she had a whole lot more—and number one was, did she want to be coached by a guy who had wrecked his family and his whole life because of his gymnastics dreams?

"Yeah," Lee agreed. "Mom still worries about him. That's why she wanted me to spend some time with him down here—so I could keep an eye on him."

"That's real big of her," Carli murmured. "So how's it working out?"

Lee managed a small grin. "Let's just say I'm still worried."

"And it's big of you to tell me about it," Carli added. "I hope you didn't mind me asking. I appreciate it."

"It's okay. I got a load of stuff off my chest," he said, starting to clear away the plates. "Hey, Carli, about this coaching stuff—it's still your choice, you know. You do what's best for you."

"Thanks anyway." Seeing Ben through the window and hearing her mom talking to her dad out at the reception desk, she knew that it was time to move.

"We're down to fifteen guests next week and thirteen the week after," Beth was saying as she consulted the reservation books. "I know it's early in the season, but that's still not enough."

"Too many bills, too few guests," Don muttered. "The same old story."

Carli sighed as she stood up and followed Lee to the corral. She felt unsettled by his story, surrounded by problems that she couldn't solve.

So where does that leave me? she asked herself. *Do I chase my dream, or do I stick with my folks and help out all I can, because it doesn't look to me like I can do both, the way Mom and Dad have me working all hours. Do I reach for the stars or keep my feet on the ground?*

"Okay, here we go—another day, another dollar," Don Carroll said, striding after Carli and fixing his dusty Stetson firmly on his head.

Feet on the ground, counting the cash, making ends meet. She sighed and then gazed up at the big blue sky. "Okay, forget it," she said. "Even if everything else was simple, there's no way my parents could afford to pay for extra coaching from Rick Scottsdale. No way in the world!"

Chapter 5

That evening Carli called Lorene.

"Hey, Carli!" Lorene sounded surprised. She turned down the background noise from the TV. "What's up?"

"Lorene, I've been thinking through what we talked about yesterday. The Rick Scottsdale idea."

"Good. Did you talk it over with your folks yet?"

"No. But listen, that's the thing. My mom and dad—you know, we don't have a lot of money. The ranch isn't doing too well right now."

"I hear you, Carli. But don't worry about that part. I've already discussed it with Rick. He says it's not a problem."

Carli felt a dart of anger run through her. "Hey, listen, I thought we were waiting until Monday before we took it any further!"

"We were," Lorene agreed. "But Rick must be a mind reader. How else do you explain the fact that he came to me this afternoon and floated the idea of taking you on as his student in the buildup to the interstate competition next month?"

"He did?" Lorene's news had completely taken the wind out of Carli's sails. She'd picked up the phone with it all planned out—*Hey, Lorene. I've been thinking through the Rick Scottsdale idea. I don't think it would work. I'm sorry, but I'm going to have to say no . . .*

"Yeah. As a matter of fact, Rick is here now, sitting in front of me as we speak. He came over an hour ago and asked me if I thought it would be a good idea if he started coaching you one on one."

"That's weird!" Carli stammered.

"Big coincidence," Lorene agreed. "I told

him right away that your folks weren't exactly loaded—I hope you don't mind, Carli. Rick said it wasn't about the money. He spotted a quality in you that could take you far."

"He did?" Carli didn't usually sound like such a dope. But this thing was speeding out of her control. All of her reasons to say no were dissolving like lumps of sugar in hot tea.

"So," Lorene went on, "as far as payment for the coaching goes, Rick is happy not to take any extra. All you have to do is pay me for the group lessons, and Rick and I will split it fifty-fifty. He won't take a cent more, and if you don't believe me, I'll put him on so you can talk to him." Her voice faded as she handed over the phone

"No, don't do that!" Carli protested loudly. Too late. Rick cleared his throat.

"Hey, Carli. Looks like Lorene and I had the same idea," he said with a short laugh. "No, really—I'd be more than happy to teach you. Actually, it'd be a privilege."

This was too much! Carli held the phone away from her ear and tried to think. *It's not just the cash we're short on—it's time, too, remember!* She held the phone close again. "I don't know, Rick. I'm really busy. I have to put in a lot of work for my mom and dad here on the ranch."

Plus, there's the backstory I got from Lee earlier. I don't want my life to fall out of balance like yours did. That would be seriously scary! But she couldn't say this straight out. It would have to lie below the surface.

"It sure is a big commitment," Rick agreed. "But you know the old saying—if you want something done, ask a busy person. I'm a believer in that."

"Well, I guess maybe I could fit in a few extra lessons during the week," Carli said slowly.

"We could take it easy at first—see if we get along," Rick suggested. "Not all coaching relationships are made in heaven. We'd have to wait and see."

Fair enough. "And you think you could help me take some big steps forward?" she asked, feeling suddenly shy.

There was a pause. Dialogue from the TV filtered through. "I could teach you what I know, and that's just about every aspect of this sport you can think of," Rick assured her, quietly confident without coming across as a loudmouth. "And I could show you the world of top-level gymnastics. We could get out to competitions, build up your confidence. Who knows where it would lead?"

To the Olympics! Carli closed her eyes, trying not to be blinded by the bright lights that beckoned. *To competing with the world's top gymnasts . . . to achieving the perfect ten!*

"Carli, are you still there?" Rick asked.

"I'm here."

"Think about it some more. Maybe

tomorrow you could come to the gym after school as usual, and while Lorene works with the group, we could split off and look at your floor exercise. We'll pull it apart and put it back together with a little more fun and personality, like I said."

Carli nodded. "Okay," she said.

"Good, see you then."

"Yeah, see you tomorrow."

"Okay, goodbye for now, Carli."

"Goodbye."

How did that happen? Carli thought in silence after she put down the phone. *Did I just get myself a new coach in spite of everything? Oh, wow, yes, I guess I did!*

"Now, Carli, you're young and you still have some growing to do," Rick said before they began.

On the other side of the gym, Lorene worked with Tanya, Gina, Martha, and the others.

"Anyhow, I think you'll stay below five-five. You'll probably build up a little additional muscle, but not too much. You're a natural ectomorph."

"I am?" Carli was nervous. She seemed to be walking through a door that she'd never been through before.

Rick smiled. "That means you're a skinny kid who doesn't easily put on weight. It has to do with genetics."

"That makes sense—my mom's small and thin."

"And you have excellent flexibility, plus stamina."

"You can tell all this just from watching me a few times?" Carli was impressed. She began to feel less scared.

"All this, plus a lot more. But what I haven't had a chance to figure out yet is what's inside that head of yours. What makes you tick, Carli?"

She stared back at him as if he was speaking a foreign language. No one had ever asked her that before. "I have no idea!" she said.

"Okay, so what makes you happy— besides gymnastics?"

She thought hard and said, "Riding bareback through Silverfish Creek. Being out alone halfway up a mountain."

"Sounds neat," Rick agreed. "Freedom, huh?"

She nodded.

"So now we can begin. Carli loves freedom. Freedom is what we have to express in the dance moves of this floor exercise. I want to see you reach for the sky."

Carli nodded and got into position for the start of her routine.

"We know you can go through the moves pretty much without fault," Rick reminded her. "That's the easy part. Now, try to capture that feeling you have out there on the mountain—with no one around. Just endless space, pure white snow, blue sky . . ."

Rick put on Carli's music and then stood back.

She took a deep breath and waited for the violins. They sounded like water running through the creek, like birds soaring overhead. She kept the pictures in her head and began.

The handsprings flowed; the Cossack leaps across the diagonal seemed to make her fly. Then the body wave—like a bird's wings spreading and lifting her high, giving her momentum for the salto and through into the slow section, as if the white-water creek had hit a smooth, slowly winding section—a little bit sad as well as calm, with the cello's deep notes pulling on her heartstrings. Her whole body swayed and bent to the rhythm; the walkover was as smooth as silk.

Rick took in every detail—the angle of Carli's head, the extension of her fingertips, the expression on her face. "Now, have fun!" he said as the music quickened again.

A bubbling stream, light sparkling on the

water, running on forever. Carli saw the picture as she went into the connected saltos. She felt the speed and the lightness as she tumbled this way and that. And now her triple twist, which should feel difficult, but this time came as naturally as breathing—a rapid sprint across the floor, leaping and twisting three times, landing with a sense of total soaring joy!

"Well?" Lorene asked when she met up with Carli and Rick after the session.

Rick didn't answer but turned toward Carli with a questioning look.

She was still breathless, still flying. She nodded and smiled.

"Good, huh?" Lorene checked with Rick.

"*Good* doesn't cover what I just saw," he told her. His normally expressionless blue eyes were lit up with excitement. "*Magic* might do it. Or try *One in a million!*"

Carli's eyes sparkled. She could hardly

believe her ears.

Lorene gave a satisfied nod, and then she put an arm around Carli's shoulder. "So at last you think you found your golden girl, Rick?"

"Maybe," he said as the elation faded and caution crept in. Then his certainty over Carli's talent broke back through. "You bet!" he said. "We're going to take this girl to Denver. She's going to be a star!"

Carli sang in the shower. Tingly clean, having changed into jeans and a T-shirt, she floated out of the changing room, down the corridor, and out into the parking lot, where she found Lee.

"How was training?" he asked.

"Cool. Your dad's an amazing coach."

Lee smiled ruefully. "Maybe I should've been a gymnast," he said quietly. "That way I'd sure have seen a lot more of him!"

"Did something just happen between you and your dad?" Carli asked.

"Yeah, he didn't show up at Pizza Hut at four-thirty. Turns out he was too busy coaching you. He forgot. Anyway, are you ready to go home?"

"Yes, but I was expecting to get a ride with Ben." She felt lousy about being the reason for Rick's no-show.

"I already called Ben to say I'd take you," Lee explained, striding off toward the jeep.

Rick shouted after Carli. "See you Wednesday at four o'clock. Balance-beam practice. Don't be late!"

Chapter 6

"What's eating you?" Don Carroll asked Carli when she and Lee arrived home.

"Nothing," she replied, striding along the porch into the house.

It had been a long, silent drive, with Lee cocooned in a shell of silence and Carli still experiencing twinges of guilt.

"Did you say thanks to Lee for the ride?" her father called after her.

"Thanks, Lee!" Carli let the door slam shut.

Inside the house her mom was at the computer, working on a balance sheet showing complex figures and columns of profit and loss. "Hey, Carli," she said absently. Then, "Shoot!" as she clicked the wrong button and her figures disappeared. "I need a break," she said, sighing.

"I'll get you some coffee," Carli offered, disappearing into the kitchen.

Beth soon followed. "How was school?" she asked wearily.

"Same old," Carli mumbled. As usual, she'd been late handing in work, and as usual, she was in trouble. "But, hey, I have good news."

"You do?" Beth accepted the coffee gratefully and then slumped in a chair. "I'm glad you do, Carli, 'cause I sure don't. I've been staring at those figures for a full hour, and no way can I get them to look okay for the bank."

"So, my *good* news," Carli persisted, sitting across the table from her mom. "I got myself a new gymnastics coach."

"You did?"

"*Hey, that's terrific news, honey! I'm real glad for you*," the rosy-cheeked voice said.

"Well, I guess Lorene actually found him

for me," Carli explained. "It's a guy named Rick. She knows him from way back."

"So why bother changing coaches?" Beth asked, pinching the bridge of her nose to ease her headache.

In her parallel universe, Carli pictured her mom bright-eyed and glowing with pleasure, eager to hear every detail. "*Go ahead, tell me all about it. This is so exciting!*"

"I'm not switching coaches exactly. Lorene will still be there, and we'll work as a team. But Rick can give me one-on-one attention. He's going to figure out a unique training program with me. I don't have to wait in line."

Beth sighed and then sipped her coffee. "Jeez, Carli. Stop right there. Before you say any more, what's this Rick guy going to charge us for the privilege of one-on-one teaching?"

"Zero. The cost is the same as it is for working with Lorene." Carli had expected this and came right in with the answer.

"How cool is that?"

Her mom shook her head slightly. "The same? How does that work?"

"Rick is asking for what Lorene gets—not a penny more."

"But, I mean, how does it work for him? Why would he do that?"

Carli had held on to her temper so far, but now she flared up. "Mom, you're so suspicious! I mean, does everyone have to have a bad reason for doing something good? Can't it just be that he likes my work and wants to help me improve?"

"Yeah, but you're still a kid and you're naive," Beth reminded her, quickly tiring of the argument. She got up to leave. "And I'm your mother, so I have to look out for you."

Carli followed her out onto the porch. "You're not saying I can't do this!" she begged. "Please, Mom, don't do that!"

"Not now, Carli. I don't have time." Beth tried to push past Carli, who stood in her way.

"Okay, okay!" Carli had to think fast. "Listen, Rick isn't just any guy. He was a top gymnast. If you don't believe me, we could Google him. He'd be up there onscreen for you to take a look at. Come back inside and see!"

Her mom hesitated. "Maybe later," she conceded.

But Carli wouldn't let it drop. She followed Beth from the porch, out across the yard toward the corral. "And here's another reason. Rick's last name is Scottsdale. Rick Scottsdale—Lee Scottsdale—get it? Rick is Lee's dad. You like Lee, don't you? So you'll like Rick, too."

Carli bit her lip. On second thought, maybe this last part was a mistake. Now she had to keep her fingers crossed that her mom wouldn't march straight up to Lee and ask him his opinion of his dad.

So she babbled on, trying to fill the silence. "And he's a really cool guy. He was an Olympic athlete way back in seventy-six, so he knows what he's talking about. Plus, he's doing it for practically nothing. What's not to like?"

Slowly, her mom's mood softened. "I hear you," she muttered.

"So?" Carli ran in front to stop her from opening the corral gate.

"So maybe I'll call Lorene to talk it through with her," Beth conceded.

"When?" Carli pestered. "Tonight, Mom. Do it tonight!"

"Later, when I have time. Now go and start your homework and give me some peace!"

"What's the worst thing that could happen while you're up there balancing on that beam?" Rick asked Carli on Wednesday after school.

So far Beth Carroll hadn't gotten around to calling Lorene to discuss the new coaching situation. On the other hand, she hadn't said no to Rick either. So, as impetuous as ever, Carli had taken this as a yes and gone right ahead.

"The *worst* thing?" she echoed, pressing the balls of her feet onto the narrow beam and standing on tiptoe. "That's easy—I could fall off!"

"And then what?" her new coach insisted.

"I get a zero point five deduction."

"What else?"

"I could break a leg, which isn't as bad as breaking my back if I fell off the bars during a high-flying release, I guess. But I still prefer the bars."

"What is it about the bars that you like? Tell me right away—off the top of your head."

"Speed," she answered. "Once I'm up there, I never stop moving."

"But on the beam you have to slow it down, strike a pose, to show the judges that you're in control?"

Carli nodded. "Too much time to think."

"Which means your natural way of doing stuff is to rush at it and use your instincts?"

"I guess." It was the first time that Carli had ever had to analyze these things, but now that Rick mentioned it, he was right on target as usual. "Thinking isn't my strong point. Ask my teachers!"

Rick grinned. "Okay, so on the beam we need to keep you moving—flowing from one move into the next. Let's start with the three-sixty-degree turn element that you just introduced. Do you want to do it on one foot or one knee?"

"The left knee," Carli decided quickly.

"Good. Then you can change level through a push-up arch into standing and then down again into a split. Let's see how that works."

No problem. Carli had listened carefully to the instruction and performed it without fault.

Rick stood back and clapped his hands.

"Carli, you were born on a balance beam, I swear!"

"Thanks," Carli mumbled, a little embarrassed by the coach's praise. "What do you want to do next? Do you want to see my one-eighty-degree leap or my forward handspring into a salto?"

"Your diet is high in protein and carbs but low in vitamins and way too high in processed sugar," Rick pointed out on the following Saturday. He'd asked Carli to write down everything that she'd eaten between Wednesday and Saturday, and now he was inspecting her sheet while the group worked with Lorene. "Where's the fruit?" he asked. "Where are the vegetables?"

"There." Carli pointed to Thursday evening. "French fries. Potatoes are vegetables!"

"Yeah, right! Listen, I'm going to put you on vitamin supplements." Rick pulled down a couple of brown plastic jars from the shelf in the treatment room. "You have to take these three times a day, with every meal. Okay, now tell me what exercise you get when you're not working here in the gym."

"How long do you have?" Carli asked. She'd already put in 90 minutes of work with Rick and Lorene on the uneven bars. The time had flown by, and yet again her new coach had been full of praise. But now she needed to shower and rush to meet her mom outside the vet's clinic.

"Plenty, huh?" Rick asked.

"Okay, let's see. I'm on horseback for three hours a day, minimum—five or six hours over the weekends and during vacations. I train the new horses. I scoop manure in the corral. I haul hay bales onto the back of the jeep . . ."

"Okay, enough. I forgot you live on a ranch. How's that moody son of mine shaping up?"

The good-natured question took Carli

by surprise. "Lee? He's cool."

"Tell him to answer my phone calls, would you? Say he's even worse than I am at keeping in touch, and I'm the first to admit I'm not the greatest."

"Sure," Carli promised halfheartedly. "But I haven't seen much of him lately either. Listen, sorry, Rick, but I have to go."

"Okay, so tomorrow would you like to put in an extra session on the vault?" he asked quickly. "Then we'll have run through all four events, and we'll do a major evaluation to see where we go next."

"If I can get a ride into town on Sunday," she agreed. "I'll call you and let you know."

Rick looked hard at her. "Or you can chill out tomorrow if that's what you'd rather do. Don't let me push you too hard."

Carli looked up to meet his gaze. Her clear brown eyes stared straight into his narrowed blue ones. "No, I want to work on my vault. I'll get a ride with Ben when he comes in for church," she promised.

"Good girl. We'll put in some extra difficulty, to increase your start values for Denver and the interstate."

"Sounds cool," she said with a nod.

"So get a good night's sleep!" Rick called after her as she sped off toward the showers.

It had been a good morning. Carli had been relaxed while she'd shown Rick her routine on the uneven bars, swinging with perfect rhythm and transferring with split-second timing from the low bar to the high bar and then back again.

As she'd told Rick on Wednesday, she loved the speed and thrill of swinging from the high bar, using the momentum to twist up into a handstand, transferring her weight, swinging down again, straight and true, gathering speed until she flipped off the bar with a perfect dismount.

But now, as she crossed Main Street and headed for the meeting with her mom outside the vet's, she knew from one look at Beth's face that the merry mood was about to change.

"So what kept you?" Beth demanded, tapping her watch. "We said noon. It's ten past."

"Sorry. Rick was running through my diet sheet with me."

"*Rick*?" Her mom searched her memory. "Oh, yeah, Mr. Nice Guy. The one who's teaching you for peanuts. Listen, I didn't speak to Lorene yet."

Carli hurried down Main Street after her mom. At times like this it was best to say nothing.

"It's way down today's list, let me tell you, after picking up these vaccination certificates from the vet, stopping in at the feed store to order more grain, taking those broken bridles into the saddler, and a meeting with the bank."

"That's okay," Carli said breathlessly. "Lorene was the one who suggested this switch, remember? She's totally fine with Rick joining the team."

Just then, a familiar tall, slim figure swung around the corner onto Main Street. It was Miss Hanson, Carli's science teacher from Springs Middle School. Also, she was an old friend of Beth's.

"Hey, Beth. How are you doing?" The teacher's greeting was friendly enough. She was clearly in off-duty mode—blond hair up in a ponytail, wearing sunglasses and cutoff jeans.

"Good, Molly. Thanks." Carli's mom was all set to hurry on until the teacher spoke again.

"Listen, I was meaning to call you and ask you and Carli to come in to school. Seems like we have the opportunity right now, if you have a minute."

Carli gritted her teeth and hung back. This was *so* not her morning after all!

"Sixty seconds flat," Beth agreed. "I have to go to a meeting at the bank."

"Poor you!" Molly Hanson grimaced and then got an earnest look on her face again. "This is about Carli's work at school. To be honest, Beth, she's just not serious about science. She owes me three pieces of work from this quarter alone. The truth is, she's falling way behind."

Beth raised her shoulders. "I hear you," she said, seemingly without surprise. "Listen, I do my best to get Carli to do her homework on time, but at her age I don't think I should stand behind her, watching her every move."

Hey, I'm here! Carli wanted to object. *Talk to me, why don't you?*

"For sure." Molly Hanson readily backed off from any possible argument in the street. Still, she hung on to her chance to talk to busy Beth Carroll. "But I was wondering what else occupies Carli's time. Is she overloaded with other stuff? Does she have enough time to complete her homework?"

"She has enough time *if* she makes time," Beth snapped back. "Listen, Molly, I have to go now. But I do understand what you're saying—Carli lacks motivation in science. It's the same with all her schoolwork. I say it to her father— 'If your daughter put just ten percent of the effort into her studies that she does into her beloved gymnastics, we'd have a child genius on our hands!'"

Yeah, lighten the mood, Mom. Turn me into a joke! Blushing bright red, Carli walked on ahead, away from the two women and across the street to where their jeep was parked.

"I thought you were coming to the bank," her mom called through the closed window when she'd finally said goodbye to Molly Hanson and caught up with Carli.

"I'll wait here," Carli mouthed back. A fear was rising up in her that was stronger than anything that she'd felt before, worse than any fear of falling from the bars or the beam.

As her mom went off through the double doors of the bank, Carli slumped down in the passenger seat. She closed her eyes and tried her hardest to take in deep, even breaths—in-out, in-out. *Control the fear. Tell yourself the worst might never happen.*

Chapter 7

"You know something, Carli? You're no fun anymore." Tanya stood beside Carli outside the round .pen at the Triple X. It was late Saturday afternoon, and the girls were watching Ben show half a dozen guest kids how to barrel race.

Carli tried to shrug off her friend's criticism. "Don't you start on me, please! Anyway, I did tell you about the Miss Hanson incident right after. Mom and I had just gotten back home, and my dad had given me a hard time about the whole school thing. I warned you not to visit if you were looking for an F–U–N afternoon!"

"Okay, I'm cool about that," Tanya agreed. "Hey, Miss H. was pretty mean, talking about school stuff off duty in broad daylight. Don't she and your mom go way back? Didn't they go to elementary school together or something?"

"So?" Carli sighed and watched a geeky, city-slicker kid race Gunsmoke between the lined-up barrels in superfast time. "Good job, Gunsmoke!" she called to the gray horse.

Tanya turned her back on the fun and games to lean against the high rails. "So, that's not the issue. What I'm saying is, why don't you lighten up now and come to Gina's sleepover like we planned? My mom will be here to pick me up pretty soon. All you've got to do is pack an overnight bag. Come on—why not?"

"Because!"

"What kind of reason is that? Come on, Carli, what's with the frowns and the sighs? It's not just Miss Hanson, is it?"

"Yeah, it is—I'm grounded because of her," Carli explained. "Mom told Dad about it, and he said no more social stuff until I've caught up with my science work. I have to get a B by the end of this quarter."

"That's tough," Tanya tutted. "So no sleepover?"

"No sleepover and no fun for me, thanks." Carli spotted Tanya's mother's car making its way down the winding track that led to the ranch. "Tell Gina I'm real sorry."

"Okay, I'm out of here!" Tanya saw the cloud of dust raised by the car tires and looked relieved. She waved goodbye and ran to meet her mom.

"And the best time in the barrel race is by Tommy Woodman on Gunsmoke at one minute, eleven seconds!" Ben yelled in the style of a rodeo announcer. "Second-best time was Macey Ingells on Columbine at one minute, twenty-six seconds . . ."

No, actually, it's not just the Miss Hanson stuff, Carli thought as Tanya jumped into the car. She saw the red brake lights wink as Tanya's mom backed up and then drove quickly back up the hill. *The problem is like a smoking volcano about to blow.*

The next morning, right after Carli had schooled Diamond, she went to find Ben in the tack room.

"Hey, Carli, you're up early," he commented. "What can I do for you today?"

"Can you give me a ride into town and back again after you're done at church?" she asked. The sooner they left, the less chance her parents would have to question her about where she was headed.

Anyway, as far as she was concerned, training with Rick didn't fall into the fun category, and so she was free to go.

Except this was Sunday and an extra session, and so she should really have checked it out with her mom.

Except again, the answer would have been a great big "no," so why risk the question?

Quit the dilly-dallying and just do it! she

told herself impatiently.

"Sure I can," Ben told her, going outside and getting into his car. "Jump in."

"Okay, the vault is a discipline where you only get one shot." Rick had been joined in the cool, empty gym by Lorene, who stood to one side as usual as he drilled Carli.

Nodding and looking apprehensively toward the apparatus, Carli thought that for some reason today the vaulting table looked higher than usual.

"You have a twenty-five step run-up, plus a single second to show what you can do," Rick reminded her. "It's about body alignment, shape, quick repulsion. Bang, and you're done!"

"Are you okay with that?" Lorene checked with Carli.

Again she nodded. *The table's not higher, stupid!* she told herself. *It's the same size it always was.*

But she was small and slight; she didn't have as much muscle as some older gymnasts. Then again, look at Nadia Comaneci when she scored those perfect tens! She was tiny and skinny. Like a small bird—light and airborne.

Okay! Carli drew herself up as tall as she could. She prepared for her run-up.

"Success in any sport is five percent talent and eighty percent sweat and tears." This had been Rick's parting shot at the end of the special Sunday morning session, and Lorene had agreed.

"What's the other fifteen percent?" Carli had asked, picking up on his faulty math.

"Science," Rick explained. "Technical stuff having to do with building the groups of muscles you need for each separate event. Eating the right diet. A little bit of physics, a whole lot of anatomical study."

He was starting to sound way too serious for Carli's liking.

"Don't worry about it," Lorene had assured her. "That's Rick's job. All you have to do is follow the program he lays down for you. Oh, and enjoy the feeling when you're doing the Yurchenko—coming backward off that table in a one-and-a-half salto and sticking your landing without shifting your feet one single inch!"

"But not yet!" Rick had cut in with a grin. "The Yurchenko comes later, Carli—when we've worked our way through the program, we've been to Denver to compete, and we're ready to take on the rest of the world!"

Now, as Ben's silver SUV jolted down the winding drive back to the ranch, Carli was beginning to feel nauseous.

What's wrong with me? she wondered. *This morning I got jittery about the vault; now I'm getting sick. What's going on?*

Once Ben had parked by the tack room,

Carli climbed out on shaky legs. *This is really getting to me*, she thought. *I'm still hearing Rick's voice inside my head— "Twenty-five steps and then, bang! Round-off entry onto the beatboard, back handspring onto the table . . ." I'm obsessing over every little detail, and it's driving me crazy!*

Out in the round pen, Lee was working with Diamond. He had her saddle on and was testing his weight in the stirrups as the filly sidled skittishly across the pen. When Lee spotted Ben and Carli, he slid to the ground and led the filly toward them. "Boss's orders," he explained. "Mr. Carroll wants to speed things up and get Diamond out on the trails by the beginning of the summer season."

Carli reached up and stroked between Diamond's eyes. "Did my dad ask where I was?"

Lee nodded. "I said I thought you'd gotten a ride into town with Ben for some extra coaching."

"Carli's really into her gymnastics," Ben commented. "Hey, Lee, I didn't know your dad was coaching her now with Lorene."

The young wrangler nodded and then strode off, leading the filly.

"What did I say?" Ben wondered, turning to Carli. "I got that right, didn't I? That was Rick Scottsdale I saw you with, coming out of the gym?"

Still the volcano didn't erupt.

Carli got through the weekend and into Monday without the drama that she was expecting—the "How could you go behind our backs?" stuff and the big showdown about school versus gymnastics.

"The more work you put in, the more rewards you get out," Rick told her at the Monday afterschool session. They were working through the floor exercise, focusing on the three connected saltos, reaching the triple twist and the high point of her routine. "You have to think of your hips as the axis of the flip—the pivot."

Carli nodded. "I see that."

"And you're tired of hearing me talk." Rick read her mood well. "You just want to do the stuff, not listen to a lecture."

"Right." She was happy with her floor exercise, except for maybe one or two small points. "I was wondering if maybe I could change the level of my movements a little more—especially in the middle slow section."

"Another relevé, maybe after the walkover?" Rick considered the idea. "Let's try it."

"The whole thing?"

He nodded. "From the beginning, one last time."

Make it good! Carli told herself. She waited for the music to lift her spirits. Then, the second she began to move, she felt the stress of the last few days slip away. She threw herself into handsprings and leaps, dancing across the diagonal, pulling off fabulous scissor kicks, using the full extent of the mat.

Rick was pleased as he noticed Carli allowing the music to take over.

"Good job, Carli!" he called as she came to the end of her routine. He called her over. "No relevé," he reported back. "It works better without it."

"Okay." Winded but happy with her performance, Carli stood with her hands on her hips.

"Listen," Rick went on. "I want us to think ahead to Denver."

Carli nodded. Her new coach sounded as serious and intense as usual.

"The competition is twelve days from now. The junior section will bring in gymnasts from across the state."

Another nod.

"I want you to really test yourself against the best in the state—to be at the top of your sport."

"I know. Me, too." This face-to-face

talk was bringing home the importance of the competition. Carli felt her stomach churn.

"It'll mean putting all your focus on training up until then. No late nights."

"As if!" Carli gave a hollow laugh. "That's no problem, Rick. I promise to get my beauty sleep!"

"So you're ready to give it everything you've got?" he asked.

Carli took a deep breath and then nodded.

"Great!" he said. "That's exactly the answer I was looking for."

When it happened, it wasn't the volcano that Carli had been dreading. No explosions, no anger, only the cold decision served up to her on a plate.

"Your mom and I have been talking," her dad began. For once he'd picked her up from the gym himself and was driving her home. The sun was setting behind the mountains, leaving a black jagged outline against a deep red sky.

Carli stole a quick glance at her father's face. His don't-mess-with-me expression was even more set than usual, his voice tight with controlled emotion.

"Mom had a phone call from your principal, Karl Mitchell. He told her about the problems you've been having at school."

"I'm sorry, Dad. I am trying to catch up in science, honest!"

"I don't want to hear it, Carli. Just listen. They talked about the problems, and your mom had to admit that good grades are not your priority—never have been. As she explained to him, not all kids are straight-A students."

Where is this going? Carli had expected another big fight, but this wasn't how it was working out.

"We knew from the get-go that you weren't the brainy type, Carli." Her dad took the dirt track toward the ranch. Years of driving the route allowed him to go perilously close to the sheer edge without putting them in actual danger. "At three years old we could put you on a horse and know you'd stay in that saddle through thick and thin. But ask you to sit for five minutes looking at a book—no way!

"That's what your mom told Mitchell. The below-average grades don't bother us. But we do kind of feel that you're wasting a lot of time in school, including the forty-five minute ride in and back again, when you're never going to be academically gifted. Plus, we need as much help as we can get running the ranch."

This was a long speech from her dad. The car swerved again. *I get it!* Carli thought with a sudden lurch of her heart as they careered along.

"So your mom and I talked it through and called Mitchell back. We told him we plan to take you out of school as soon as we can, which is the end of the week."

"And then what?" Carli cried. She leaned forward and braced both arms against the dusty dashboard as the jeep jolted and her life turned upside down.

"Then we homeschool you," her dad replied calmly. "Your mom will direct your studies at the ranch from here on in. That'll be it until you're old enough to quit."

Chapter 8

Carli cried herself to sleep. She woke up crying.

This homeschooling stuff isn't about me getting better grades, she thought as she ate breakfast in silence and her mom and dad carried out their normal ranch chores. *For starters, how will Mom find the time to teach me properly? No, this is about making life easier for them, getting me to work more hours for them.*

The way Carli saw it, this was definitely the way it stacked up, and she cried some more as her dad drove her to school.

The second she walked into the building, Tanya noticed that her eyes were red and puffy.

She pulled Carli over to one side. "Time to share," she told her firmly.

Carli shook her head. "If I talk about it, I'll fall apart."

"Go ahead, fall. I'm here to pick up the pieces."

"It's *so* not fair." Carli's lip trembled, but she held back the tears. "This should be the best time of my life. I have a new coach. He thinks I'm good enough to do well in Denver next week. I should be on cloud nine!"

"But?" Tanya dragged Carli into the privacy of the girls' bathroom. "What's gone wrong?"

"Everything! My mom and dad—that's what went wrong!"

"I hear you. Sometimes I feel like that, too—like this morning, when Dad wouldn't let me wear mascara to school. He made me wash my face and come barefaced!"

Carli's strangled laugh turned into a sob.

"They're going to homeschool me, starting next week," she blurted out. "I have to quit Springs Middle School this Friday."

"Oh, my gosh, Carli!" Tanya grabbed her arm. "When will I see you? I mean, will you still come to gymnastics? Please say yes!"

"I don't know," Carli confessed. "I guess they haven't told me about that yet. And I'm too scared to push it."

"But you have to come. What about Rick and Lorene? They won't let you stop. You're way too talented!"

"Thanks, Tanya." Carli ran the cold water and washed her face to get back in control. "Don't tell anyone else what I just told you, okay?"

Tanya nodded. "You know me—Tanya Velcro Mouth!"

"I don't want everyone to gossip. I want to slide out of here on Friday without making a big deal."

"You're shaking!" said. "Are you sure

you're okay to go to class?"

"I'm cool," Carli said, holding her head high as they went out into the corridor.

Wednesday was Carli's last science class. After class, she stayed behind to hand in her books.

At first Miss Hanson didn't look her in the eye. "You can leave them on the shelf," she said, turning her back. Then she rethought her uncaring mode. "Listen, Carli—I hope your parents' decision to take you out of school wasn't just because of me."

Carli had her guard up, like she'd had since her talk with Tanya two days before. "No way, Miss Hanson. My folks just think homeschooling is the way to go from now on. It's not like it's a big deal or anything."

"Fine. Only, I do realize it will take you away from your friends, with you living such a long way out of town and all."

"That's okay. I'll have more time to train

the horses. That's what I want to do with my life after I'm through with school." *Let me out of here before I fall apart*, Carli thought. She was putting so much effort into putting on this front that her whole body had started to shake again.

"Honestly? I heard it was gymnastics that you were into," Miss Hanson said. "Will you still be able to do that when you're being homeschooled?"

"I guess," Carli answered, as casually as she could manage. "But gymnastics doesn't last forever, does it? I mean, it's not something to hook all of your life on, let's face it!"

"How did Carli do today?" Lorene asked Rick following Wednesday's coaching session on the beam, after Carli had rushed off to catch her ride home with Ben.

"It's not her best event." He shrugged. "But this kid has iron willpower. She makes herself focus, even when she's not having a great time up there."

Lorene listened carefully. "Yeah, but however strong willed she is, there's something different about her lately. Less 'bounce,' as you call it. Did she say anything to you?"

Rick shook his head. "We worked on the routine. She did what she needed to do to prepare for Denver at the end of next week. We didn't talk."

"But something's definitely wrong," Lorene said thoughtfully. "In the past the one thing you could rely on with Carli is that she'd dismount from the apparatus or finish her floor exercise with a grin spreading from ear to ear!"

At home, whenever she had a few minutes free from ranch chores, Carli worked on the program of exercises that Rick had given her to build up extra upper-body strength. At school she got through her last week with only Tanya knowing her secret. On Friday she went through the gates for the final time.

"I'm *so* going to miss you!" Tanya's feelings spilled out of her as she and Carli walked through town. "We've been going to school together since we were six years old, for Pete's sake!"

"I'll miss you, too," Carli confessed. Her stomach felt tight and weird and her brain wasn't taking things in the way that it should, so nothing was fitting together and making sense.

Was this really it? What was going to be the pattern of her life from now on?

"But I'll see you at the gym tomorrow?" Tanya asked anxiously. "Tell me you'll be there!"

Carli's head swam as she nodded and said goodbye. She still hadn't broached the subject at home. "There's Mom, waiting for me outside the bank. I have to go, Tanya. See you later—bye!"

"Did you hand over all your books?" Beth asked on the drive home.

Carli nodded.

"And you said your goodbyes? Did you thank your teachers, Carli? I hope you did. After all, this homeschooling decision has nothing to do with the quality of their teaching. They worked hard with you, and I wouldn't want you to be ungrateful."

Disconnected from what her mom was saying, Carli stared out the window as they drove past the trailer park on the outskirts of town.

"I wrote away for the homeschooling program that's appropriate for your age," Beth went on. "We should get it on Monday. I'll free up some time, and we'll begin right away."

"Whatever," Carli said with a sigh. She didn't want to talk about it—about how the Triple X would be her whole world from now on, how her future was set in stone. Schoolwork would be way at the bottom of the list, beneath scooping manure and hauling hay bales and maybe training horses if she was lucky and her dad was in a good mood once in a million years.

And where did gymnastics and the competition in Denver fit into that?

Beth glanced over at her silent daughter. "You know, your dad and I are convinced that this is the right way to go," she insisted. "You remember Luke Coles? His folks have been homeschooling him since he was ten. They think it's worked out pretty well. And then there's Hayden Meakin over at Blue Mountain Ranch. She goes to college next year, and she's been homeschooled all her life up to now."

Carli closed her eyes. *Let me wake up and find out this is a bad dream!* she prayed. *Make everything go back to the way it was!*

Early the next morning, Lee came knocking at the ranch-house door.

Carli opened it. She had hardly slept or eaten for two whole days. Rick's diet sheet had been shoved to the back of a bedroom drawer.

"How does your first day of freedom feel?" Lee asked. "No school for you from now on, I hear!"

"That's true," she muttered. "It feels weird."

"Hey, you want a ride into town?" Lee asked. "I have to collect the mended bridles and pick up a new pair of spurs for myself. I'll be leaving in ten minutes."

"No thanks," Carli told him. "I'm skipping gym class today. I'm sick."

"I can see that." Lee studied her pale face and red-rimmed eyes. "What's up?"

"My stomach—I don't feel good."

"Huh. I'm sorry to hear that. Did you call my dad?"

She shook her head. "Can you do it for me, please? Listen, I have to go now."

"Where?" Lee was worried. Carli was never sick. In fact, she was the healthiest kid he knew.

"Back to bed," she whispered, closing the door and dragging herself up the stairs.

"Carli, Rick Scottsdale is on the phone!" Half an hour after Lee's visit, Beth called upstairs. "I'm busy with breakfast. Can you come down and talk to him?"

It was the last thing Carli wanted to do. She'd rather crawl under a rock and never come out, not face things, avoid everybody. But Rick was hanging on at the other end, demanding answers.

"Hey," she said weakly into the phone.

"Hey, Carli. Lee says you're sick."

"Yeah, sorry, Rick. I won't be able to make it."

"So did you call the doctor?"

"No. My stomach is upset. I'll be okay soon."

There was a pause. "So what's the real problem?" Rick asked. "What are you holding back?"

"Nothing, really!"

Another pause. "Lee also tells me your folks took you out of school."

Deep breath. "Yeah, that's right."

Right to the point. "So how will you get into town for coaching from now on?"

Silence.

"Carli? Are you okay? We're a team— you, me, and Lorene. You should've told us. Listen, we'll figure this out. Don't let it get to you, okay?"

A nod of the head that Rick couldn't see. Tears began to roll down Carli's cheeks.

"Hang in there, Carli. Let me talk to Lorene. Then, after the morning class, we'll drive out to the ranch and sit down with your folks. Do you hear me? We'll keep coaching you, whatever happens. Just stick with it—okay?"

Chapter 9

Rick's words calmed Carli. She was part of a team. She wasn't alone.

"Hey, how about getting dressed?" Her dad was passing through the house when he noticed her still in her PJs. "Ben needs help in the corral."

There was no "Why aren't you in town getting coached?" or "Do you feel okay?"

"I'll be there," she promised, going upstairs to get changed. She even managed a mouthful of breakfast.

"Too late," Don grunted when she showed up. "The morning trail ride already left for Sawtooth Lake. Ben had his hands full, I can tell you."

Feeling the full force of her dad's putdown, Carli swept out the tack room, watching the clock and counting the minutes until Rick and Lorene arrived.

"Lunchtime!" Beth announced just before noon.

The riders were back in the corral, tying up their horses, happy with their morning's ride.

Carli forced down a chicken sandwich, checked her watch again, and then looked out for Rick's car on the steep driveway.

But the only car raising dust on the track belonged to Lee. He drove too fast and screeched to a halt outside the tack room, ignoring Carli as she ran out to meet him.

"Lee!" she called.

But he didn't stop to talk. Instead, he strode into the bunkhouse and shut the door.

And Carli was growing edgier by the minute as another hour passed and her coaches still didn't put in an appearance.

Rick shouldn't have promised what he couldn't deliver, she grumbled to herself. *It looks like he talked to Lorene and she's not in agreement. She's telling him to let it drop— no way can they keep coaching me if I can't get into town!*

She'd started the day at her lowest point. Rick's promise had raised her. But now she was down, sitting on the floor again.

"I want to keep doing gymnastics," she told Diamond as the chestnut filly stood in the feed stall munching grain. "I do! Sure, it can be scary, and it's a whole heap of hard work, especially with Rick giving me a tough time over all the technical stuff. But it's what I *do!*"

And now she saw herself—a lithe, slim figure pounding toward the beatboard, springing onto the table, twisting through the air. She felt herself swing like a pendulum from bar to bar, releasing and then catching, twisting, and swinging again.

"I do it well!" she told the unconcerned filly. "When I'm up on the bar, my balance is one hundred percent as steady as a rock. When I'm doing my floor exercises, I flip and twist and fly like a bird!"

I don't want to stop, she told herself, feeling her confidence flow back, banishing her blues. *I want to go to Denver, I want to compete, and I want to win!*

"Carli? It's me—Lorene."

The phone call came at three o'clock. Carli's mom had rerouted it from the house to the tack room, where Carli took it into the tiny, chaotic office full of dusty papers and odd bits of broken tack.

"What happened?" Carli demanded. "Why didn't you and Rick come out to the ranch?"

"That's why I'm calling." Lorene sounded hesitant. "Something bad has happened."

"It's okay, no need to tell me," Carli jumped in, her heart thudding with disappointment. "You two talked and decided it was too complicated for me to keep training. That's okay—I can handle it."

"No, Carli—listen!"

"Like I said, I can handle it. No need to explain."

"It's not like that!" Lorene insisted. "I want you just to listen. Something came up with Rick. I still can't believe it!"

"It's Rick!" Carli was worried. "What happened to him? Is he okay?"

"Yeah, he's okay," Lorene assured her. "He's not hurt or sick or anything. But he's in a tight spot right now. I just went to see him, and he said I should go ahead and tell you what happened."

"You went to see him where?" Carli demanded. A big black fly buzzed at the cobwebby office window, trying to escape. "What did he say you should tell me?"

"You need to sit down," Lorene warned. "Okay, Carli, brace yourself—Rick's in jail. The sheriff arrested him."

"You're kidding!" Carli gasped. "Tell me this is a joke, Lorene."

"Listen. Rick was seen driving into the gas station next to the mall. It was around eleven, just after he and I had talked and decided to drive out to the Triple X. Rick said his car needed gas. He planned to fill up the tank while I finished my class. Apparently, he did this and then stepped inside to buy a newspaper.

"Only, according to the attendant, he had no intention of paying for the paper. If you believe what the guy told the sheriff, Rick gave him some wild story to distract him, reached into the cash register while his back was turned, and stole around a thousand dollars. He ran off without even stopping to get his car!"

"That doesn't make sense!" Carli protested. The trapped fly flew straight at her, and she brushed it aside. "Rick wouldn't do that!"

"I know. But the attendant, even

though he was new in the job, was still able to give the sheriff a description, and it matched Rick. Plus, there's the car still sitting there." Lorene finished with the facts and then sighed. "If it's true and Rick truly was short of cash, why didn't he come to me? I'd have helped him out with the money, no problem."

"I know, I know." Carli was still reeling. "What happens now, Lorene?"

"It looks like they have enough evidence to charge Rick with theft."

"But they can't—he wouldn't!"

"I'm sorry, Carli, but that's the way it's heading." Lorene waited for a few moments. "Listen, I can still drive out to see you if you like. I can come by myself and explain a few things to your folks."

"No," Carli muttered quickly. "No thanks, Lorene. There's no point."

"You're sure?"

"Yeah, I mean, if Rick's in jail and he's guilty, I lose my chief coach."

"I know . . . I'm truly sorry!"

Carli took a deep breath to steady herself. "It's okay, Lorene. And listen, I know this is a small thing compared with what Rick's going through. But without him as my coach, there's no way I'll get to Denver next week!"

Carli drifted through the rest of the warm afternoon in a dejected daze. Just before five o'clock, she bumped into Lee in the empty corral.

He stopped to lean against the barn door, head hanging, his face hidden by the brim of his Stetson and looking as if the world had come to an end.

Carli went up to him. "Did you hear the news?" she asked quietly.

Lee looked up and nodded. "Lorene called me and told me where Dad ended up."

"I'm shocked!" Carli said.

"Yeah. I was worried about him, but even I didn't think it would end this way."

"No, I mean that I don't believe it. There must be some mistake."

"You sound like my dad," Lee said, sighing. "That's what he's telling the sheriff—it's a mistake, he didn't do it, yak-yak! But from what I hear, they caught him red-handed."

"Lee, this is awful . . ."

"I'm so disappointed," the young wrangler admitted, his voice hardly more than a whisper. "I hoped this move to Colorado would be a new start for him, but now look what's happened."

"Stop!" Carli didn't want to hear. She made Lee step inside the barn, where it was shaded and private. "If your dad says he's innocent, I believe him. So should you, 'cause you're his son! He never did anything like this before, did he?"

Lee shook his head. "He may have done a heap of crazy stuff, but he was never dishonest or in trouble with the law."

"So why start now?" Carli argued. "Just

when he's set to take me to competitions and turn me into the star he's always wanted to discover? You said yourself—it's what he wanted to do since way back."

"Yeah." Lee frowned. A small glimmer of hope showed in his eyes. "You know, maybe there is some mistake . . ."

"For sure! Okay, so you've lost sleep over Rick," Carli admitted. "But when you two do meet up, I can see there's a lot of love there between you, even if you don't show it . . . Hey, what am I saying?"

"What is it?" Startled, Lee took Carli by the shoulder. "Come on, what's on your mind?"

"I just realized something. You—you're always thinking negative stuff about your dad. When you drove back here at noon, you were banging doors and ignoring people. Had you just run into Rick before you left town?"

"What if I had?" Lee asked. "It doesn't help with this arrest stuff. Let's try to stick to the main point here."

"But this *is* the main point!" Carli argued. "You two met up just before you drove home, is that right?"

"Yeah. So?"

"So what time was that—can you remember?"

"Around eleven, maybe eleven-fifteen. I ran into him on Main Street, right outside Annie's Bakery, but he just about cut me dead—said he had to go and get gas, but he couldn't remember where he'd parked his car, so he had no time to talk. The same old stuff."

"And you arrived here at noon." As far as Carli could see, this all added up. "Listen, Lee, Lorene told me the robbery happened right then—right at the time when you saw your dad trying to find his car!"

Lee stared. "Are you sure?"

"Certain!" she cried, grabbing him by the arm and pulling him into the yard. "And there will be witnesses at Annie's to back you up. Come on, Lee, we've got to go!"

★ ★ ★

"You folks can visit," the sheriff told Lee and Lorene, "so long as you don't object to my leaving this door open so I can listen in. But you stay in the office with me," he told Carli.

Lee and Carli had driven into town. Their first stop was to pick up Lorene. The second stop was the town jail.

"But I want to see Rick!" Carli protested.

"Sit!" the sheriff told her.

So she sat. She watched Lorene and Lee walk through to the next room. Through the open door, she spotted iron bars making a partition between prisoners and visitors. Carli shuddered to think of Rick locked up behind them.

"Okay, Rick," Lorene began without any beating around the bush, "what exactly happened this morning, after you left me to get gas?"

"I never made it," he told her. "I walked

out into the parking lot to where I left my car, but it wasn't there. For a minute or two, I thought I was going crazy."

Keeping her ears open, Carli threw a glance at the sheriff, who sat turning and tapping his pencil against the desk.

"You couldn't make this up!" the sheriff told her with a cynical wink. He was in his 50s, with a papery, wrinkled face and a worn expression that said he'd been on the job way too long.

"What next?" Lorene prompted Rick.

"I thought maybe I'd gotten it wrong—that I'd left my car outside my house and walked over to the gym to see you. I wasn't sure—I thought I'd had a senior moment, maybe. So I headed off down Main Street."

"Which is where you ran into me," Lee put in. "And you cut me dead."

The sheriff's pencil stopped in midair. His expression grew more alert.

"Right!" Rick confirmed. "But I never found my car, Lee, I swear. It wasn't outside my house, so I ran back to the gym parking lot to double-check, and it wasn't there either."

"Could somebody have stolen it?" Lorene asked quickly. "That's what I'm figuring, Rick—that the guy who robbed the gas station stole your car first."

"Huh!" the sheriff looked like a tracker dog whose ear was pricked. "That would explain why the car was left there—to incriminate Scottsdale."

". . . I guess that could be true," Rick told Lorene uncertainly. "The only thing I know for sure is I never drove that car to the gas station. I never stole the money!"

"And here's Lee to prove it," Lorene insisted. "Are you listening to this, Sheriff?" she yelled through the doorway. "Are you writing it all down?"

"Yeah, Dad, you were with me!" Lee declared in a loud voice. "I'm your alibi!"

Chapter 10

"It turns out the guy at the gas station was in on it," Lee explained to Don and Beth Carroll back at the ranch.

News of Rick Scottsdale's arrest and subsequent release had spread like wildfire around the small town. Now, late on Saturday evening, Lee was telling his bosses the full story while Carli stood impatiently in the doorway.

Outside in the yard her two coaches sat waiting in Lorene's car, though Carli's parents didn't know yet that Lorene and Rick had come to see them.

"The attendant and the guy who actually pulled off the robbery planned it together. They set up my dad because he looked like an easy target—someone new in town, a drifter, looking like his luck was running out. They knew he didn't have too many friends around. So one guy steals his car and drives it to the gas station. The attendant gives my dad's description as the guilty party. The car is there as evidence."

"A mean trick," Don grunted. "How long did Sheriff Perry take to get the full story out of those two guys?"

"Approximately sixty seconds," Lee grinned. "They caved in the minute he knocked on their motel-room door and showed them his search warrant. The stolen cash was stashed in a bedside table."

"Thank goodness," Beth said with a sigh. "And you were the hero, Lee. Walking in and giving your dad an alibi."

"If I'm honest, that was down to Carli," he admitted. "She was the one who put the pieces together and came up with the explanation for what happened. My dad and I really want to thank her."

"My dad and I." Carli loved the sound of those little words coming from Lee's mouth.

"My dad and I owe you a lot," he'd told her on the ride out to the ranch in the setting sun. "My dad and I plan to take a vacation after the case goes to court and those guys are locked up behind bars." *My dad and I.*

"So now you can stop worrying and have a cool time with your dad," she'd told him. "Happy ending."

It had taken a crisis to make this happen, but now Carli could look at Lee's relieved, happy face as he talked about Rick and know that it had been worth it.

Beth Carroll looked like she was thinking hard, struggling with a feeling that she couldn't put into words. "How about some coffee?" she said briskly as Lee finished his story.

"Can you make enough for Lorene and

Rick?" Carli cut in as her mom made her way to the kitchen. "They're waiting out in the car."

"Carli, what are you thinking?" Beth's good manners kicked right in. "Why are they out there in the dark? Ask them to come in!"

"Yeah, why are they here?" Don echoed, opening the door and calling in the visitors.

Carli's heart missed a beat. *Clunk* went the car doors. Footsteps crunched across the yard.

Don Carroll shook Rick by the hand. "You must be mighty proud of your son."

"Likewise," Rick replied. "You have a fine daughter, Don. Without Carli, I'd still be behind bars!"

Enough of this proud-parent fest! Carli's jitters grew worse by the second. *Get down to business, please!*

"Lorene, come in. How do you take your coffee?" Beth asked, returning with a heavy tray. "Carli, I made you hot chocolate.

Sit down, everyone. Relax."

So they sank into the leather couches, the lamps around the room shedding soft pools of light on the paintings of cattle roundups on the walls and the hide rugs on the floor.

"So, Beth, we need to talk about your daughter's future," Lorene began. "At this moment Carli has a big question mark hanging over her."

Thump-thump-thump! Carli could feel her heart pumping.

"She does?" Beth turned to Carli with mild surprise. "You do?" she asked.

Carli couldn't answer. She had to let Lorene and Rick do the talking.

"The bottom line is—Carli is an amazing gymnast," Rick told Don and Beth. "She has incredible talent—something I expect to see only once or twice in my life."

Thump-thump, quicker and quicker. Carli clenched her fists.

"Hey, Carli, that's good to hear," Don said.

"A talent like this needs careful nurturing," Lorene insisted. "We need to figure out with you how we're going to take Carli forward, which includes the basic stuff about how she gets into town for her coaching sessions now that she's no longer at Springs Middle School."

Crunch time! Carli's heart practically burst through her ribs—it was thumping so hard.

"We didn't consider that yet," Don said slowly. "Carli, you didn't talk to us about it."

She shook her head. "You were busy, and I was scared it wouldn't work out," she confessed. "My head was a mess. Sorry."

"Don't be sorry," her dad muttered, deep in thought.

"I was wondering, when you made the decision to homeschool, did you think through all the angles?" Lorene said softly.

Don glanced at Beth. "We sure didn't consider the gymnastics issue," he conceded.

"And I guess I didn't calculate exactly

how much time I'd have to spend on the teaching," Beth added. "Since I looked at the program, I'm starting to think it's way beyond my capabilities!"

Carli looked from one to the other. At first she couldn't compute what she was hearing. Was this really the sound of her parents backing down?

"So you'd be happy to put Carli back in school?" Don checked with his wife.

"If you agree," Beth said, nodding.

"Okay, that's settled. I'll call the school first thing on Monday."

"Wow!" Carli came out with that same jaded, pathetic word. Nothing else fit the miracle that had just occurred.

"So, what's the answer to the other main question?" Lorene asked bluntly. "Does Carli get to continue with her gymnastics coaching?"

Don Carroll looked at his wife.

"You have a big, big talent, Carli!" Beth said, as the realization dawned on her that her daughter was something special. "Hey, Carli, why didn't you tell us how good you were?"

"Because she's a modest kid who doesn't go around shooting her mouth off," Don cut in quickly, turning to Carli. "That's right, isn't it? It's how we brought you up."

She nodded. "But you knew how much I live my life through gymnastics. You knew that."

Quietly, her parents said yes, they did. They remembered she loved to somersault and tumble over the furniture as a little kid. They recalled how she'd spent most of her time as a five-year-old walking on her hands, cartwheeling on the lawn, and standing on her head in the hay barn.

"So, honey, you get to continue your coaching," her dad said firmly. "We'll fit it in around your school and ranch chores, no problem."

"Yesss!" Carli leaped out of her seat and punched the air. Then she sank back with an almighty sigh.

"And listen, Carli," Lorene went on, "Rick and I were talking on the way out here. We've seen enough in this last couple of weeks to know that we need to step back and let you *enjoy* what you do, not load you down with technical stuff."

"Me especially," Rick agreed. "I get too caught up in the details. I don't see the bigger picture, as Lee here can tell you."

Lee gave a wry grin. "As Carli already knows," he explained to Beth and Don, "my dad is a little obsessive about his work. Always has been."

"But learning not to be," Rick assured him.

"And he's good," Lorene added. "The best coach around."

There was a pause then, with all eyes settled on Carli, everyone slowly reaching their own conclusions.

"I guess I know what it's like to take work too seriously," Don admitted after a while.

"It makes you blind to the important stuff under your nose—like your family and how much you love them."

Say that again, Dad! Carli could hardly believe her ears.

"You love them and you take them for granted," Don went on. "You expect too much."

It was Beth who cried, not Carli, though Carli felt as if sharp, icy splinters were finally melting inside her heart.

"We should be sorry, Carli," Beth sobbed. "Not you."

"Don't cry, Mom. Everything's okay," Carli whispered.

"So, Carli, you get to work hard with us and have fun," Lorene declared, seeing that it was time to go. She stood up and moved quickly toward the door.

"And we're going to get ready for Denver," Rick promised. "Starting tomorrow morning, with an extra session to make up for lost time."

"Tomorrow at nine!" Carli agreed. "I'll be there!"

"And I'll give you a ride in!" Lee, Beth, and Don all chimed in at once.

"What makes you happy?"

It was the most important question that Rick would ever ask Carli, even though they were to work together at both national and international levels for the next six years.

Wild water and snowy mountains. A red-tailed hawk soaring overhead.

She drew on these images now as she waited to begin her floor exercise, already happy with her high scores on the vault, the uneven bars, and the beam.

The sports stadium on the outskirts of Denver was the biggest she'd ever seen; the faces of her mom, dad, and Lee were small blurs in the audience on the far side of the floor.

"You've put the work in, and now you

can show those judges what you can do," Carli's dad had told her before the final event.

Her mom had squeezed her hand and turned tearful again.

"You go, girl," was Lee's parting shot.

Now Carli was a tiny figure in a blue and silver leotard standing under a huge, brightly lit dome. Her dark hair was tamed into a high ponytail, and she held her hands by her sides. Her head was high.

I'm here! she thought. *This is me—Carli Carroll. I made it!*

Her music began.

It sounded like water running over rocks, like spray splashing and sparkling in the clear air.

Carli threw her slight body into a series of handsprings. She leaped higher than ever before. Her body wave was as lithe and sinuous as willow branches in the wind.

Then she changed direction, flipping and twisting across the floor with perfect rhythm and timing, waiting for the deep strains of the cello to draw her into her sequence of slow moves, like an eagle soaring, like the slow echo of voices calling down the mountain valleys.

Living each second, being in the moment, spinning, turning, twisting, and sprinting into the triple twist, high in the air in a moment of pure happiness at what her body could do.

Carli waited for the judges' scores. Lorene sat on one side, Rick on the other.

All of the competitors started the exercise with a score of nine. The judges would make deductions for every flaw and weakness. They added value for difficulty, up to a maximum score of ten.

"Carli Carroll—we saw powerful tumbling in all directions," one judge said during their private assessment.

"Smoothly connected saltos," another noted. "And there was real personality at play."

Still in the dark, Lorene put an arm around Carli's shoulder and kept her fingers crossed.

Rick was confident. He'd put movements in the routine that gave two level "D"s and one level "E." None of the other competitors had that. But still, you could never predict how the judges might react.

At last, they punched in their numbers, and the giant scoreboard lit up.

10. 10. 10 . . . Carli looked along the row.

Rick and Lorene jumped up from their seats. The audience broke into a roar of applause.

Perfect tens!

"Congratulations, Carli," the voice on the loudspeaker announced. "A new star is born!"